P9-BZS-141

I CAN'T BELIEVE IT'S HISTORY! FUN FACTS FROM AROUND THE WORLD

By Katy Keck Arnsteen and Donna Guthrie

Copyright © 1993 by Katy Keck Arnsteen and Donna Guthrie
Published by Price Stern Sloan, Inc.
11150 Olympic Boulevard, Los Angeles, California 90064

Printed in the United States of America. All rights reserved. No part of this publication may be reproduced, stored in a retrieval system or transmitted, in any form or by any means, electronic, mechanical, photocopying, recording or otherwise, without the prior written permission of the publishers.

ISBN: 0-8431-3621-9
10 9 8 7 6 5 4 3 2 1

Dedicated to Bernard Margolis and the Pikes Peak Library District Librarians.

PRICE STERN SLOAN
Los Angeles

RUB-A-DUB-DUB

"Rub-A-Dub-Dub, Three men in a tub." Not always. There was a time when bathing wasn't very important to people.

Early baths were found in Crete. King Minos built a great bath in his palace and brought water to the royal tub through terra-cotta pipes.

The Greeks loved to take baths. They thought it was healthy to take short, cold baths after exercising. Their baths were next to the gymnasium where they played sports.

The Romans liked their baths long and the water hot. Public bath houses were open from noon to night so bathers could get clean, relax and talk. They piped the water in from the sea and took saltwater baths.

 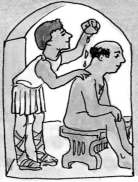   

Shower or bath?

What's the best way to get clean?

Showers are considered more refreshing but if you want to get really clean, take a bath!

The Roman bath was divided into five stages each with its own room. First, a bather would exercise to get warmed up and then enter a warm room where he would sweat a little with his clothes on.

In the second room, he would undress and have slaves rub him with special oils.

Next came a hotter room where he would sweat some more and relax in a hot pool.

Then he would go into the hottest room of all where slaves poured lots of cold water over him.

In the last room he would jump into an ice-cold bath.

Bathing like this took hours and lots of water. The average Roman used 300 gallons of water a day.

During the Middle Ages, it is said that Europe went a thousand years without a bath.

After Pope Gregory in 1085 A.D., baths were allowed again.

The monks heated water and carried it to the tub. The eldest monk bathed first followed by the others, all using the same water. The youngest bathed last, just as the water turned cold.

In towns, cleanliness depended on how rich you were. People used their fingers and ate from a common pot, so hand washing was very important.

People covered up their dirt and body odors with makeup and heavy perfume.

The whole world wasn't dirty. In Japan, people enjoyed bathing and were extremely clean. Women and men took baths together, a practice which Westerners found shocking.

In the late 19th century, people began to understand that being dirty caused disease.

London built public bath houses where people could go to bathe. In between baths they used lots of perfume.

In America, mixed bathing wasn't allowed. Public baths had rooms for men and women with separate entrances. Next door to the bath houses were public laundries so people could use the leftover water to wash their clothes.

When portable tubs were invented, people took their baths on Saturday night. Houses didn't have running water. Instead, water was heated in the kitchen and carried to the tub. One tub full of water was used by the whole family.

Now tubs are built next to a tiled wall with indoor plumbing. Average Americans spend about 11 minutes in the shower or 20 minutes in a bath. Compared to the early Romans who bathed for hours, we pull the plug much too soon.

No one knows when or where people first made soap. Romans used soap 3,000 years ago. In the late 1700s, a French scientist found that lye could be made from table salt. This made soap much cheaper, so everyone could afford it.

PAT-A-PANCAKE

When you sit down for pancakes, did you know you're eating something that's 800,000 years old?

Archaeologists have found stones which primitive people used for grinding grain. The pictures on the wall show people eating pancakes. They are probably the world's oldest kind of bread.

The early pharaohs of ancient Egypt ate pancakes; they were part of their everyday diet.

The early Greeks had a recipe for pancakes which used eggs, flour and milk—just the same as today.

Long ago people celebrated spring planting and harvest time by eating pancakes.

In the early Christian church during Lent, a time of fasting, people were not allowed to eat meat, eggs or milk. So on Shrove Tuesday, the Tuesday before Lent, they mixed up all their eggs, milk and butter with a little flour and made pancakes.

The English celebrate Shrove Tuesday with pancake races and pancake-eating contests.

Native Americans made pancakes with corn meal instead of flour.

In France, February 2 is Pancake Day. One custom is to toss a pancake into the air with one hand and catch it in a pan while holding a piece of money. The French believe that this will bring the pancake flipper good luck the whole year through. Sometimes a thread is hidden in a pancake and the person who finds it wins a prize.

In the Netherlands, people create gigantic, oven-baked pancakes and decorate them with icing.

The Dutch brought pancakes to America in the form of the "Dutch Baby," a giant flat-topped popover. Early settlers practically existed on some form of pancake calling them flapjacks, journey cakes and hoe cakes.

Jack is an old English term for a half-cup liquid measure. A flapjack was a half-cup of fruit enclosed in a pastry flap and fried. In Colonial America, fruit was mixed into the batter. Over time, the fruit was left out and "flapjack" became just a pancake.

Journey cakes were a basic food for hunters, prospectors and settlers moving west. Pioneers used the flat blades of their hoes and cooked pancakes over the open fire. Topped with molasses or jam they were delicious.

The most famous tall tale of pancakes is about Paul Bunyan. He was the biggest, smartest, strongest lumberjack who ever lived. Paul hired armies of woodsmen to clear the forests of the mid-west. Legend has it that the bunkhouse cooks couldn't flip flapjacks fast enough to satisfy all the hungry men. So Paul built a colossal flapjack griddle which was greased by men with slabs of bacon attached to their feet. Every time they wanted to flip the pancakes, they blasted the griddle with dynamite!

Mexican tortillas, Chinese Mandarin rolls and French crepes are all different versions of the pancake.

Today we can buy all different types of pancake mix in boxes. Or you can mix your own batter. For a nutritious breakfast, you can experiment by adding berries, diced fruits or seeds and nuts to make a breakfast fit for a pharaoh!

BASIC PANCAKES

1 cup all-purpose flour
1 tsp. baking powder
1 tbsp. vegetable oil or melted shortening
1 egg
1 cup milk or water

1. Mix all the dry ingredients in a bowl.
2. Combine the liquid ingredients together and beat well.
3. Combine the two mixtures together.
4. Pour about 1/4-cup batter into a lightly greased hot pan. Cook until set, about 1 minute. Turn over and cook the other side until done, also about 1 minute.

This recipe makes about 8 six-inch pancakes.

HOLD ON TO YOUR HAT

There's no such thing as a new hat. Hats have been around since early man covered his head from the sun and the rain. Hats told a man's place in life. You wore your hat with friends, tipped your hat to a lady and took off your hat for the King.

Ancient Greeks wore hats only when traveling to protect them from the sun. Their hats were made of felt or straw.

The Babylonians wore hats with high crowns and turned-up brims.

The Egyptians liked wigs and didn't want to clutter them with headdresses or hats. Often they wore simple gold bands around their heads or a long linen scarf.

Cavalier   Merchant   Peasant   Artist

In the Middle Ages, a man was known by the shape of his hat. You could tell if a man was a doctor, a lawyer, a priest or a student by looking at his head gear. If you wore the wrong hat, it was called a "falsehood."

Make a newspaper hat of your own.

Hat Language

To take up a collection is "passing the hat."

To "keep something under your hat" is to keep a secret.

And talking "through your hat" means you're saying something silly.

Isabelle of Bavaria arrived in France to marry Charles VI and brought the "hennin," a cone-shaped headdress draped with a veil. Other women followed the fashion and the cones grew taller and taller. Europe had to redesign doorways to fit these high-hatted women.

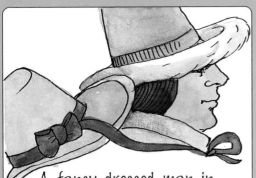

A fancy-dressed man in the 14th Century wore two hats—a tall felt hat on his head, and a second hat tied over his shoulder or on top of his walking cane.

In Colonial America, people took their hats very seriously. The Puritans passed laws saying only the rich could wear fancy hats.

Over time people have worn all kinds of things on their heads. Imitation bee hives, caged birds and mice were once fashionable.

In the old west, a cowboy found many uses for his hat, a wide-brimmed hat with a high crown. He could start a campfire by fanning the blaze, carry water to his horse and wave it at an angry bull.

Today some hats tell us about our clubs and hobbies. Some hats are worn only during certain seasons or occasions. Police, fire fighters and the military wear hats to tell us what jobs they do.

A modern hat designer would have to be very imaginative to outdo the hat of the Chieftain of the Mayans in 1502 A.D. It was made of feathers, gold and precious stones.

Bonnet

Turban

Top hat

Twin-horned escoffion

Tam

Straw hat

Some Hats Through the Ages

Coolie hat

Two-cornered hat

Sombrero

Stocking cap

EAT 'EM UP

Knives, forks and spoons weren't always used to bring food to our mouths.

Early man ate with his fingers. Meat, berries, fruit and fish went from hand to mouth.

In the Stone Age, men used flint knives to cut meat into pieces. Sticks were used to cook it over the fire.

Five thousand years ago, around the Mediterranean, people used spoons made of sea shells, sometimes fastened to a handle of bone or wood.

An early spoon from around 3000 B.C. was found in Switzerland. It was carved from wood.

Other spoons were made from horns. Curved horns of sheep or goats made good spoons.

Early Egyptians made bronze spoons with a sharp handle. One side for spearing and the other side for scooping.

Chopsticks in China

By 400 B.C., people throughout China used chopsticks. These two sticks, 10-to-12 inches long, are held in one hand and used to pick up bite-sized pieces of food. The Chinese also developed a flat-bottom spoon for soup.

A Confucian saying:

"The honorable and upright man keeps well away from both slaughter house and kitchen, allowing no knives on his table."
Confucius thought if people saw animals being killed they wouldn't want to eat them. Knives were a reminder of the killing and shouldn't be on the table.

Romans also used spoons. They thought evil spirits lived inside fresh eggs. So before they ate the egg, they pierced the shell to let the spirits out.

In the Middle Ages, people returned to eating with their fingers. They used four-day-old bread called "trenchers" as plates.

Diners kept a finger extended so that the grease could drip. Maybe that's where our custom of holding out the little finger when using a spoon or drinking tea comes from.

Travelers in the Middle Ages carried their own table utensils because innkeepers didn't provide them. The wealthy had a special case to hold their knives, but poor people just kept them in their belts.

Table utensils were so prized that starting in the 1200s, they were listed in wills and handed down from one generation to the next.

In Scandinavia, men carved spoons of wood to give to the girl they wanted to marry. Sometimes there were two spoons joined by a flexible wooden chain.

Today's formal table setting consists of a salad fork, a dinner fork, a table knife, a steak knife, a teaspoon, a soup spoon and a butter knife. To surprise your family, set the table this way tonight.

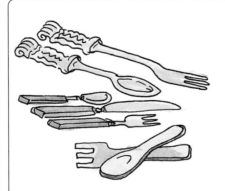

Today we have factories making eating utensils from fancy silver to stainless steel to plastic. There are all types of tableware from the very expensive to the disposable.

Fast food of today brings us back to finger food: hamburgers, hot dogs, french fries, sandwiches, tacos, pizza, pickles and popcorn. We're eating with our fingers just like early man.

BOO!

Halloween is the scariest night of the year.
How and why did it get so spooky?

Almost 2,000 years ago, the Celts, who lived in what is now Great Britain, celebrated Halloween night. The Celts believed that on October 31, Samhain, the lord of the dead, gathered all the souls of the people who had died that year. On that night he let them return to earth.

When the Romans conquered the Celts in 43 A.D., they combined the Celtic festival of Samhain and their autumn festival. The Romans honored Pomona, goddess of fruits and trees, with apples. That's why apples have become a part of Halloween.

The custom of going from house to house and asking for food may have come from Ireland. In olden days, people paraded to honor the god, Muck Oila. The leader of the group wore a long white robe and an animal mask.

Halloween became known as the night of the witches. There were good witches who were wise and used their knowledge to help people. But there were also stories about witches using their powers for evil.

Black cats became a part of Halloween because people thought witches could turn into black cats.

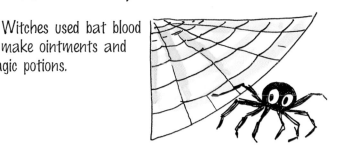

Spiders became tangled in the Halloween web because witches believed spiders helped them weave their spells.

Witches used bat blood to make ointments and magic potions.

It was thought that witches could also change into owls.

In Scotland, people paraded through the fields carrying torches. They lit huge bonfires to scare away any low-flying witches.

In France, children beg for flowers on October 31 to decorate graves for All Saints Day on November 1.

Pumpkins

In Mexico, families celebrate on November 1 and 2, the Days of the Dead. Children receive cakes and candies. People shoot off firecrackers and flares so that souls can find their way in the darkness.

Halloween became popular in the United States during the late 19th century. It was a time for children to dress up in costumes and go "trick or treating."

The jack-o'-lantern, which represents the human skull, was first set out to scare off evil spirits. The Celts thought skulls were lucky charms. In Scotland, a turnip was originally used to make a jack-o'-lantern. Turnips grown in the United States were too small to hold a candle, so pumpkins were used instead.

For a special treat, save your pumpkin seeds after carving your jack-o'-lantern. Wash the seeds, spread them out on a cookie sheet, sprinkle with a little salt and bake in a low oven until crisp.

PAPER, PAGES AND PRINT

Why was paper invented? People wanted to communicate ideas and keep records and stories.

Paper fills the world. Boxes, cards, tickets, cups, newspapers, bags, ribbon, posters, magazines and especially books, like the one you are reading, are made of paper.

From early times, people memorized stories and told them aloud from generation to generation. Sometimes story-tellers painted symbols on their bodies to help them remember.

Early man drew stories on the walls of their caves, using pictures to show a battle or a hunt. They made their own colors from plants and charcoal.

Ancient Sumeria, which is now Iraq, developed the first writing called cuneiform. They marked on wet clay tablets with sharp pointed sticks called styluses, making symbols for words. Then they baked the tablets in the sun to harden them.

Then the Sumerians discovered that each symbol could represent a sound. This was the start of the writing system we use today.

Hardcover books were made by the Mayans in 899 A.D. Descriptions tell of accordion-pleated paper made from bark which was glued to covers of brightly decorated wood. The Aztecs had similar books using picture-writing called a "codex."

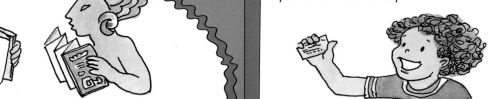

Go to the library today and sign up for a library card. With your card, you can borrow any book that you want. Its like having thousands of books for free.

The ancient Egyptians wrote their alphabet of hieroglyphics, another type of picture writing, on papyrus, which is a reed that grows along the Nile River.

They cut the reed, dried it and put strips side by side, gluing them to make long sheets. They were pressed and rubbed smooth with shells. The long rolls were called scrolls.

Scribes in Egypt would write for people who didn't know how on scrolls using reed brushes and ink. The rolls were stored in jars to protect them. Can you imagine a library of jars?

In China, Tsai Lun worked for 16 years to develop paper. The process was kept a secret. Shhh! He used the bark of the mulberry tree broken into fibers and pounded into a sheet.

By the 10th century the Chinese used wood or clay blocks to print books—which were also scrolls.

Parchment was used in Europe. It was made by stretching animal skins very thin, treating them with lime and rubbing them with rocks.

In the Middle Ages, monks copied words by hand. This took lots of time and was very expensive. Only the rich or churches could afford to buy books. Today these manuscripts are very valuable.

A German silversmith named Johann Gutenberg invented moveable type in 1450. This made the printing of books cheaper and faster and led to the printing press we use today.

Gutenberg's Bible

The Koran

Aztec religious teaching

A Megillah, one scroll from the Torah

Early books were very precious and usually reserved for sacred writing and holy manuscripts.

The largest English dictionary is the Webster's New International Dictionary, published in 1986. It defines 470,000 words with 99,943 illustrations.

The smallest book measures 1/25 inch by 1/25 inch. It was printed in Great Britain and is the story of "Old King Cole." The pages have to be turned with a needle.

APPLE CORES

The apple is one of the most popular fruits in the world.
An apple tree may live for over 100 years and grow to over 40 feet.

No one knows exactly when man began eating apples. Legend tells us that Eve gave Adam an apple. But the Bible only refers to it as the "forbidden fruit." If it was an apple, it was probably small and bitter.

Adam's apple

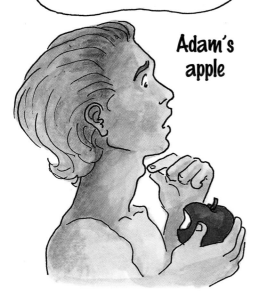

Whether or not the apple was the "forbidden fruit," some people believed that a piece of the apple got stuck in Adam's throat.

Prehistoric man ate apples that resembled the wild crab apples of today. They weren't very sweet or juicy.

In the Stone Age, people began drying apples so they could be eaten all year round.

Although apple trees grow from little seeds, the Greeks began developing better apples around 300 B.C. by using the grafting method. Grafting is attaching two plants so they will grow together.

The Romans brought the apple to Europe and England when they traveled about conquering the world and creating their empire.

William Tell

Legend tells us that William Tell shot an arrow through an apple balanced on top of his son's head to prove his archery skills to a tyrant.

In the Middle Ages, apples were popular and orchards grew throughout Europe.

Europeans brought apples to America, where the colonists planted them. They soon became "as American as apple pie."

In some countries it is an old custom to plant an apple tree upon the birth of a child. As the tree grows, so will the child.

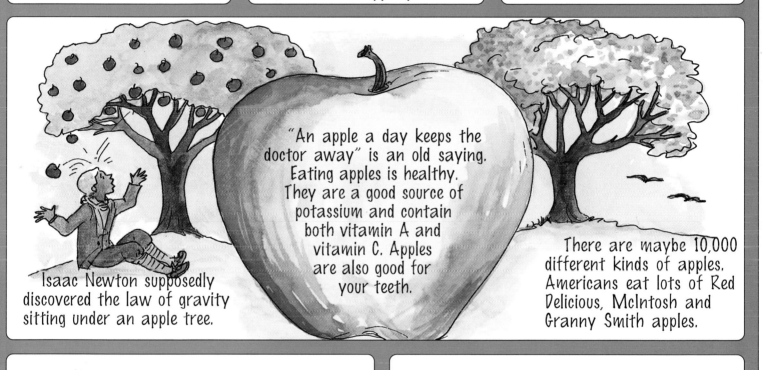

"An apple a day keeps the doctor away" is an old saying. Eating apples is healthy. They are a good source of potassium and contain both vitamin A and vitamin C. Apples are also good for your teeth.

Isaac Newton supposedly discovered the law of gravity sitting under an apple tree.

There are maybe 10,000 different kinds of apples. Americans eat lots of Red Delicious, McIntosh and Granny Smith apples.

Johnny Appleseed planted apple seeds in Ohio, Indiana, Illinois and Pennsylvania from 1795 to 1845. His real name was John Chapman and some say he wore a pot on his head, slept outdoors, loved animals and was a vegetarian.

Make a nutritious apple snack. Core an apple and remove the stem and seeds. Fill the apple with peanut butter and raisins. Cut the apple in quarters for a delicious treat.

ONE, TWO, BUCKLE MY SHOE

You take about 18,000 steps a day. During your lifetime your feet will carry you 250,000 miles wearing slippers, sandals, moccasins, boots, tennis shoes or high heels.

Early man didn't wear shoes. He went barefoot in summer and wrapped his feet in animal skins or tree bark when it was cold.

The Egyptians were the first to wear sandals. Dinner guests took off their shoes and had their feet washed before sitting down to eat. Egyptian kings were sometimes buried with sandals of solid gold.

In ancient Greece people went barefoot at home, but wore sandals outdoors.

The Romans wore sandals like the Greeks but color was important. Rich people painted their shoes.

Buckskin boots were worn by Roman soldiers marching from place to place. The Romans liked footwear and had sandals and shoes to match each outfit.

In China, it was once customary to bind young girls' feet to make them as small as 3-to-4 inches. "Lily feet" were considered a great honor because they would bring a high marriage price.

In Europe during the 1300 and 1400s, people wore leather and velvet shoes with long pointed toes. Sometimes the shoes went two feet beyond the big toe. Called "crackowes," the pointed toes were stuffed with hay or moss. To walk, the points were lifted or tied to the ankle or knee with chains.

In England, the king made laws about shoes. So common men wouldn't be mistaken for nobility, their shoes could be no longer than six inches. Noblemen could have shoes as long as they wanted.

When Henry VIII ruled England, he wore wide, duck-billed shoes. Because people wanted to look like the king they stuffed their shoes with moss to make them look wide.

From early Rome to today, men have added "lifts" to their shoes to make them look taller.

Clogs were worn first to protect footwear because streets were wet and dirty. Venetian women wore "chopines" or clogs which were 4-to-12 inches high.

In North America when the colonists arrived, the Indians wore moccasins. The colonists soon exchanged their heavy leather shoes for this New World footwear.

In early America, shoes were expensive and made by hand. It took a cobbler a day to make one or two pairs of shoes.

In the 1500s men began wearing high heels. The short French King, Louis XIV wore high heels with frilly bows. In the 1700s, men's heels were made smaller and the shoes were decorated with buckles instead of bows.

In the mid-1800s, sewing machines were invented. These machines made shoes faster and less expensively. High-button shoes required a special tool called a buttonhook just to fasten or unfasten the fourteen buttons.

In many Asian countries, it is customary to remove your shoes at the door before entering.

Try this at your house to keep the floors clean.

CLOWNING AROUND

Clowns have amused us and made us laugh throughout the ages. People have always loved entertainers who could juggle, tumble, dance, play musical instruments and trick us.

Early clowns performed short plays known as mimes, little stories from everyday life. In Roman mime, the bald fool wore a peaked hat and was known as "stupidus."

Early mimes were very talkative. Silent mime was invented by an actor who lost his voice at the height of his career.

After the fall of the Roman Empire in 476 A.D., all theaters and circuses closed. Clowns traveled from town to town spreading gossip and bringing news.

In the Middle Ages, clowns performed in the streets. They were a popular attraction at markets and town fairs.

In rich homes, a jester was kept as a part of the household to tell stories and amuse the lord of the castle.

Court jesters entertained the King. Some were dwarfs while others were highly skilled athletes.

In Medieval times, masked mummers were peasants who dressed up and performed skits, dances and tricks at fairs and festivals.

During the 16th century, the Commedia Dell'Arte was a group of actors who studied to be actors and clowns. They wore masks and costumes and performed for Kings and Queens all across Europe.

So that the audience knew who the clown was in each play, a clown would paint his entire face white. Whiteface has been part of clowning ever since.

The Harlequin is a traditional comic character who wears a mask, multicolored spangled tights and carries a wooden stick.

The early circus was a circular riding rink featuring horseback-riding tricks. Clowns stopped the program with silly acts.

The circus arrived in America in colonial times. American clowns wore white makeup, ruffled collars and bells on their peaked hats.

As the circus grew to three rings, clowns went back to performing mime. Costumes and makeup varied for each clown.

Clowns exaggerate expressions to be funny. Look in the mirror and see how you can exaggerate your expressions.

The talents of actor Charlie Chaplin made film clowning an art form. Television clowns on children's programs continue the art of clowning.

Native American tribes enjoyed clowns also. In the late 19th century, an Assiniboine Indian formed a society to perform the Fool's Dance, complete with a long stick of ribbons, bells and a whistle.

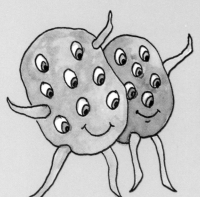

ONE POTATO, TWO POTATO

What stays in the dark and grows a hundred eyes?
No, it's not a monster from outer space. It's a potato.

The Incas grew potatoes in South America thousands of years ago. From the potato, they created a floury white substance called chuno.

On cold nights, potatoes were scattered on the ground so they could freeze. In the morning, the Incas would stomp on the potatoes to get out all the water. Then the potatoes were dried so they could be stored and used later.

Conquistadors went to South America looking for gold and silver but found the potato and took it back to Spain. The English explorers brought the potato to England and Ireland.

Europeans were slow to use the potato. They thought it wasn't fit to eat.

It wasn't until about 1721 that the potato became popular. Antonine-Auguste Parmentier created tasty dishes like potato soup.

In 1620, John Smith planted potatoes in the colony of Virginia. George Washington planted potatoes at Mount Vernon and Thomas Jefferson served them at Monticello.

During World War I, American soldiers who were in Belgium bought a fried potato snack and named them French fries.

Potatoes belong to the nightshade family of plants along with red peppers, tomatoes and petunias. Nightshade is a bitter poisonous juice.

Europeans liked the potato because it was a nutritious food which could be raised on small farms. One acre of potatoes could feed four times as many people as an acre of rye or wheat.

Ireland became famous for potatoes. The cool rainy weather was good for growing potatoes. The Irish people ate 8-to-12 pounds of potatoes a day and little else.

But in 1845, a blight attacked the Irish potato crop. Many people starved and nearly a million Irish people came to America to escape the potato famine.

Potatoes can be used for lots of things. Potato starch is used in the production of paper, glue, and lipstick.

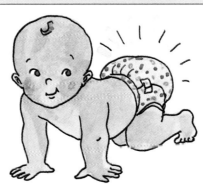

Even babies can use potatoes. From the lowly potato comes a superabsorbant biodegradable material that is used in disposable diapers.

Today the Russians are the world's number-one producer of potatoes and the Chinese are number two.

Potato Chips or Saratoga Chips were created in Saratoga, New York, when a young chef became angry over a customer's demand for thinner fried potatoes.

Souffle potatoes originated in France when a train was late in arriving for a formal banquet to christen a railroad line. A hotel chef who had been keeping fried potatoes waiting, plunged them into boiling fat a second time and to his amazement they puffed up. An accident that made a delicious potato dish!

Put an old potato with eyes into a glass of water and watch it grow!

HERE KITTY, KITTY!

Cats have been around for a long time, sometimes loved and sometimes hated.

The bones of the African wildcat have been found in caves where ancient man lived. Were they eaten or kept as mouse chasers?

The manul is larger than the domestic house cat. This long-haired feline came into the world around 2 million B.C. It is still found in Russia, Tibet, China and Afghanistan.

The cat became a household pet by 3000 B.C. and protected Egypt's large grain supply from mice.

The Egyptians worshipped cats and thought them to be household gods. They always put aside a portion of their meal for their cats.

When a cat died, the owner went into mourning and was required by law to shave off his eyebrows. Many of these cats were embalmed and mummified.

Cats move so quietly. Put a bell on your kitty so you know where he is at all times.

Bad Luck

Black cats are thought to be unlucky in many cultures. In the Middle Ages, black cats were often burned alive because they were thought to be friends of witches.

Good Luck

The Japanese Bobtail has a short curled tail like a rabbit's. When seated, it often raises one front paw. This gesture is considered good luck.

Roman mosaic of cat

Early Romans brought their tame cats from Egypt. The followers of Diana, the goddess of the hunt, worshipped cats.

The term "to let the cat out of the bag" comes from country fairs when tricksters put cats in bags and sold them as pigs. When the buyer got home, he would find out he was tricked when he "let the cat out of the bag."

The cat with no tail!

Legend has it that the Manx was late getting on the Ark and caught his tail in the door just as Noah was closing it.

Cats were on the Mayflower when settlers sailed from Europe to North America. The colonists carried cats on board to protect the food supply from mice.

The Korat cat is rare even in its native Thailand. The name means "good fortune."
A pair of these lucky cats was a traditional gift to Thai brides.

The cat has always been the rat's enemy. In 1961 the rice fields of Thailand were overrun with rats. Cats were parachuted in by the hundreds and the crops were saved.

Cats wore earrings in ancient Egypt. Bronze statuettes show cats with gold ornaments attached to its ears.

TICK-TOCK

Have you ever noticed that when you're having fun how quickly time goes by? When you're waiting for something or have nothing to do, time seems very slow. That's one of the strange things about time.

The Babylonians studied the movement of the sun and created the first clock, the sundial. A stick was put into the ground to measure the sun's moving shadow.

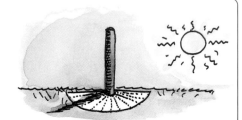

You can make your own sundial. Make a half circle out of cardboard and divide it into 12 numbered parts. Put it on the north side of a stick in the ground and watch the shadow move.

Ancient Egyptians also divided the day into 12 parts and kept track by using tall granite columns called "Cleopatra Needles." The shadow from the sun fell on 12 marks around the column.

The Egyptians also developed a more portable timekeeper using a triangular piece of wood or metal called a "style," which worked like a mini-sundial. The problem was that sundials only worked when the sun was shining.

Portable clocks

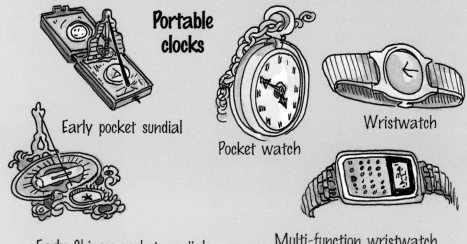

Early pocket sundial

Pocket watch

Wristwatch

Early Chinese pocket sundial

Multi-function wristwatch

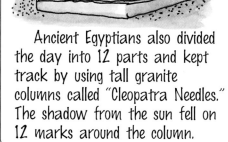

Five hundred years after the sundial, the Egyptians found another way to tell time, the water clock. This was a pot with a hole in the bottom. Since it always took the same amount of time for water to empty out of the pot, people could tell the hour by checking the level of the water. But in cold weather, the water could freeze.

Around the year 250 B.C., sand replaced water and the hourglass was invented. But if the weather was damp, the sand got stuck.

The burning candle was added to early timekeeping devices. The candle grew shorter at a steady rate, but this was an expensive way to tell time.

In the Middle Ages, people decided to replace water and sand with weights, chains, gears and springs to make mechanical clocks showing time on a face using a dial pointer.

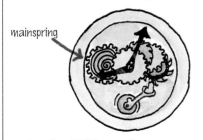

mainspring

In the 1500s, a German named Peter Henlein created a mainspring for clock makers. This mainspring was a tightly coiled spring that would unwind slowly. Because of this small spring, clocks could be portable.

The town guards carried small clocks on a strap to time their watch. These clocks were called "watches" after the men who watched the city.

The first mechanical clocks were found in cathedral towers. Because clock towers were so tall, the entire village could see the time and hear the chimes ring.

Italian scientist Galileo studied the movements of a hanging lamp. He could see the lamp moved back and forth at a certain speed. He thought that a pendulum could regulate the movements of a clock.

In 1656, a Dutch man named Christian Huygnes designed the pendulum clock after studying Galileo's ideas.

Our most accurate clock is an atomic clock in Boulder, Colorado.

In the 1600s, Mary Queen of Scots had a watch shaped like a skull. To see the dial, she turned the skull upside down and the jaw opened.

WHAT'S IN A NAME?

Don't call my name! Early societies have believed that words are magical. To utter someone's name could cast a spell on him.

In Egyptian mythology, the goddess Isis turned the sun god Ra's saliva into a snake that bit him. To escape death, Ra had to tell Isis his secret name, which gave her power over him.

In Australia, in some native tribes, every man has two names. One is secret and not known by the uninitiated in the tribe.

In Mongolia and Asia some Kirghiz tribes had rules that forbid a woman to say the name of her own husband aloud—or even a word that sounds like it.

One of the first things that happened to you when you were born is that you were given a name.

Your first name, or "given name" is called your proper name. Your last name is your family name and is called your surname.

Some Native American tribes believed their names were part of them. If anyone pronounced their name in a bad tone, their bodies would actually suffer.

In a Congo tribe, you cannot pronounce a man's name if he is fishing or he may not catch a fish.

Some parents name their children after someone famous hoping they will "live up to the name," and they sometimes do!

"A good name is more valuable than money."
—Maxim Publilius Syrus
1st Century B.C.

Most of the Chinese immigrants who came to America didn't change their names. Most of them came from the province of Kwangtung and their names go back two thousand years. The most common names are Chang, Wong and Lee.

Pseudonyms

1. Mark Twain
2. Dr. Seuss
3. Lewis Carroll

A pseudonym is a made-up name used by authors. Can you guess the real names of the authors above?

1. Samuel Clemens
2. Theodore Seuss Geisel
3. Charles L. Dodgson

Some famous names...

1. Madonna
2. Kareem Abdul-Jabbar
3. Malcolm X

Are really...

1. Madonna Louise Ciccone
2. Ferdinand Lewis Alcindor
3. Malcolm Little

Nicknames

A nickname is a name that is a shortened version of a proper name, like Tom for Thomas. Some names have several nicknames. Elizabeth has Beth, Betty, Betsy, Liz, Lisa and Eliza. Can you think of more?

Other nicknames tell about a person's looks, personality or how someone feels about them. One person may have several nicknames.

A humorous or elaborate nickname is called a sobriquet. "The Greatest" is the sobriquet of boxing champion Mohammed Ali, whose original name is Cassius Clay.

Many surnames started as definitions of one's work like Baker, Mason, Goldsmith or Hunter.

Other surnames developed from place of origin. Don Palermo's family probably came from Palermo.

In Scandinavian countries names indicate relationships. The son of Carl was called Carlson. Norwegian explorer Eric the Red's son was Leif Ericson.

Some names may have started as physical descriptions. Blackbeard wasn't blond and Longfellow must have come from a tall family.

TOYS, TOPS AND TEDDIES

Blocks, balls, hoops, dolls, rattles—children throughout history have turned objects into toys and sources of amusement and learning.

In early times, gourds were used for rattles, bones were used for dice and stones were used as balls.

Even in ancient Egypt there were balls, pull-toys, rattles and spinning tops.

Although the yo-yo came to the United States from the Philippines, it was actually a toy used in ancient Greece.

All cultures had toy "weapons" that children played with. Native Americans had miniature bow and arrows. Sling-shots, pea-shooters, wooden swords and toy soldiers are common even in peace-loving societies.

In early Crete, they had painted clay figurines. One from 1600 B.C. is of a girl on a swing—the first mechanical toy.

All cultures have had building toys:

Blocks Sand Sticks Clay

All cultures have had musical toys:

Mayan whistle Drums Rattles Bells

Certain toys that come from Asia have a very long history. Cards, kites, dominos and balloons are all from the Far East.

The rocking horse may have developed from wooden horses on wheels used to train knights in the Middle Ages.

Dolls were made of clay, wood and rags stuffed with straw.

The medieval "wind-mill" toy may be the forerunner of our modern pinwheels.

Native American mothers hung wooden hoops and balls over a baby's cradle to amuse the baby.

The Sioux took such pride in their beaded artistry that they even created beautiful dresses for their children's dolls.

Pioneer children made and played with corn husk dolls. They built toy log cabins with corncobs.

Be as clever as pioneer children and make your own toys from household objects.

paper airplane

toilet-paper roll robot

sponge fish for your bath

Once when President Theodore Roosevelt went hunting, he saw a bear cub but didn't shoot it. Newspaper cartoons appeared everywhere telling the story. Morris Minton, a toy-shop owner saw the article and created a stuffed toy brown bear. He asked President Roosevelt if he could name it "Teddy's Bear" and the President agreed.

MAKING FACES

Throughout history we have painted our faces. Both women and men have used makeup.

Jars of makeup have been found in the tombs of the pharaohs. Ancient Egyptians were buried with their cosmetics. They thought they would need them in the next life.

Beauty queens in early Egypt shaved off all their hair, even eyebrows, and wore wigs. They painted their eyelids green and used a black powder called kohl on the their eyes.

In early Babylon, young men painted their faces with white lead and a bright red dye. They curled and perfumed their hair and used oil to kill the lice.

In Persia, men stained their beards, hair and eyebrows with a reddish-brown dye called henna. They curled their beards and made them longer by adding fake hair.

In India, women painted designs on their cheeks—stars, suns, birds and flowers. They also dyed the tips of their fingers and the soles of their feet a copper red.

In African cultures, warriors and hunters of the tribe decorated their faces to look fierce.

Native Americans used face paint when they went to war and for special ceremonies.

In the early 1500s, women wanted to be pale. They painted their faces with white lead paint which was very harmful because it caused tooth decay. When their teeth were gone, women put corks in their mouths to keep their cheeks from sagging.

The Roman Beauty Bath

Poppae, Nero's wife, had over 100 slaves just to help her with her beauty routine. Each night she covered her face with thick mud which dried overnight into a hard mask. In the morning a slave would wash her face with donkey milk because she thought it kept her young.

Poppae and other Roman women wore special makeup at home called their "domestic face." She covered her skin with white chalk and drew black eyebrows that met at the nose. She painted her fingernails with red dye called "dragon's blood."

In the Middle Ages, women wanted to be very pale. They painted their faces white, often putting one coat of paint on top of another without washing their faces. This covered up the dirt.

Queen Elizabeth I liked to wear red wigs and paint her face white. When she didn't bother to look into the mirror anymore, her servants painted her face for her. Just for fun, sometimes the servants painted her nose bright red!

In the French court, patches were the fashion. A silk patch near the lip was considered very flirty. A heart-shaped patch on the forehead was dignified. Court ladies wore 7 or 8 patches at a time and carried a box full in case they lost one.

Along with patches, women made their eyebrows fuller by wearing mouse skins. A woman would only need to set her mousetrap at night to have thick full eyebrows in the morning.

The Victorian ladies wanted to look natural and wore almost no makeup at all. They wanted their skin to be pale so they wore large hats and carried parasols whenever they went out in the sun.

We have learned that too much sun is not healthy for the skin. We now use sun-blocking oils and lotions to protect our skin from the rays of the sun.

Today, we want our skin to look healthy and clean. Beauty doesn't come from a jar, isn't drawn on with a pencil or applied with a brush. Real beauty comes from inside by being healthy and happy.

Paint your face with a smile...a happy grin. And everyone will see the beauty within!

This book is published by

PRICE STERN SLOAN
Los Angeles

whose other splendid titles include such literary classics as

Awesome Facts to Blow Your Mind

Gross Facts to Blow Your Mind

Scary Facts to Blow Your Mind

Weird Facts to Blow Your Mind

Scary Stories for Sleep-overs

More Scary Stories for Sleep-overs

Still More Scary Stories for Sleep-overs

and much, much more!

They are available wherever books are sold or
may be ordered directly from the publisher.
For more information call 1-800-421-0892.

PRICE STERN SLOAN
11150 Olympic Boulevard, Los Angeles, California 90064